DIGITAL PLANET

WHAT ARE APPS?

by Nikole Brooks Bethea

pogo

Ideas for Parents and Teachers

Pogo Books let children practice reading informational text while introducing them to nonfiction features such as headings, labels, sidebars, maps, and diagrams, as well as a table of contents, glossary, and index.

Carefully leveled text with a strong photo match offers early fluent readers the support they need to succeed.

Before Reading

- "Walk" through the book and point out the various nonfiction features. Ask the student what purpose each feature serves.
- Look at the glossary together. Read and discuss the words.

Read the Book

- Have the child read the book independently.
- Invite him or her to list questions that arise from reading.

After Reading

- Discuss the child's questions. Talk about how he or she might find answers to those questions.
- Prompt the child to think more. Ask: Do you use apps? If so, what apps do you use? What do you use them for?

Pogo Books are published by Jump!
5357 Penn Avenue South
Minneapolis, MN 55419
www.jumplibrary.com

Library of Congress Cataloging-in-Publication Data

Names: Bethea, Nikole Brooks, author.
Title: What are apps? / by Nikole Brooks Bethea.
Description: Minneapolis, MN: Jump!, Inc., [2020]
Series: Digital planet | Includes index.
Identifiers: LCCN 2019001226 (print)
LCCN 2019001725 (ebook)
ISBN 9781641288958 (ebook)
ISBN 9781641288934 (hardcover: alk. paper)
ISBN 9781641288941 (pbk.)
Subjects: LCSH: Application software—Juvenile literature. | Computer programming—Juvenile literature.
Classification: LCC QA76.76.A65 (ebook) |
LCC QA76.76.A65 B484 2020 (print) | DDC 005.3—dc23
LC record available at https://lccn.loc.gov/2019001226

Editor: Susanne Bushman
Designer: Michelle Sonnek
Content Consultant: Sarah McRoberts, Human-Computer Interaction Researcher

Photo Credits: photka/Shutterstock, cover (phone); Monkik/Shutterstock, cover (screen); studioloco/Shutterstock, 1 (girl); nixki/Shutterstock, 1 (screen); Alexey Boldin/Shutterstock, 3; goir/Shutterstock, 4 (background); Stepan Bormotov/Shutterstock, 4 (ball); Oleksandr_Delyk/Shutterstock, 4 (sunscreen); garagestock/Shutterstock, 4 (screen), 14-15; Chinnapong/Shutterstock, 5; Agencja Fotograficzna Caro/Alamy, 6-7; PR Image Factory/Shutterstock, 8-9 (background); Kolonko/Shutterstock, 8-9 (screen); Samuel Borges Photography/Shutterstock, 10; hocus-focus/iStock, 11; charnsitr/Shutterstock, 12-13; Basar/Shutterstock, 16l; 24Novembers/Shutterstock, 16m; Keith Homan/Shutterstock, 16r; Africa Studio/Shutterstock, 17 (background); Andrey_Popov/Shutterstock, 17 (foreground); zhu difeng/Shutterstock, 18-19l; Photographee.eu/Shutterstock, 18-19r; mikkelwilliam/iStock, 20-21; Oleg GawriloFF/Shutterstock, 23.

Printed in the United States of America at Corporate Graphics in North Mankato, Minnesota.

TABLE OF CONTENTS

CHAPTER 1
Discovering Apps 4

CHAPTER 2
Using Apps 10

CHAPTER 3
The Future of Apps 16

ACTIVITIES & TOOLS
Try This! 22
Glossary 23
Index 24
To Learn More 24

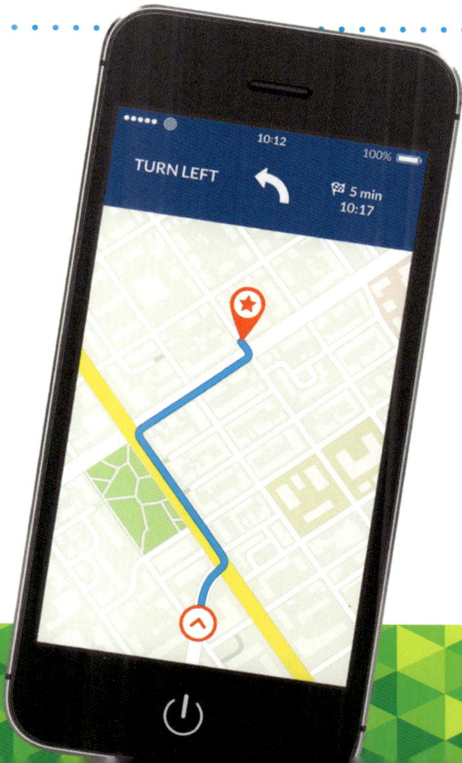

CHAPTER 1

DISCOVERING APPS

Let's go to the pool! Will it be sunny? We check the weather **app**. How do we get there? A mapping app finds the best way!

We use apps daily. But what are they? They are **software programs**. They are most often used on **mobile devices**. Like what? Tablets, smartphones, and smartwatches are some.

We download apps from the internet. We find them in app stores. Different devices have different stores. Why? Devices have **operating systems**. Each runs its own version of apps.

DID YOU KNOW?

Apple opened their App Store in July 2008. About 800 apps were available then. The App Store now has more than 2 million apps!

App Store

code
import java.util.Scanner;
public class EvenOdd {
public static void main(String
Scanner reader = new
System.out.print(
int num = reader.nextInt();
if(num % 2 == 0)
System.out.println(num +
else
System.out.println(num +
}

Some apps are free. Others must be purchased. When you buy an app, the **developer** makes money. Why? He or she created the app.

Apps are written in **code**. Code is instructions for the device. Developers write it in special languages.

DID YOU KNOW?

In 2018, 194 billion apps were downloaded. People spent $101 billion in app stores.

CHAPTER 2

USING APPS

Apps can do many things! Runners use them. Why? Apps can track **data**, like speed. They can map running paths, too.

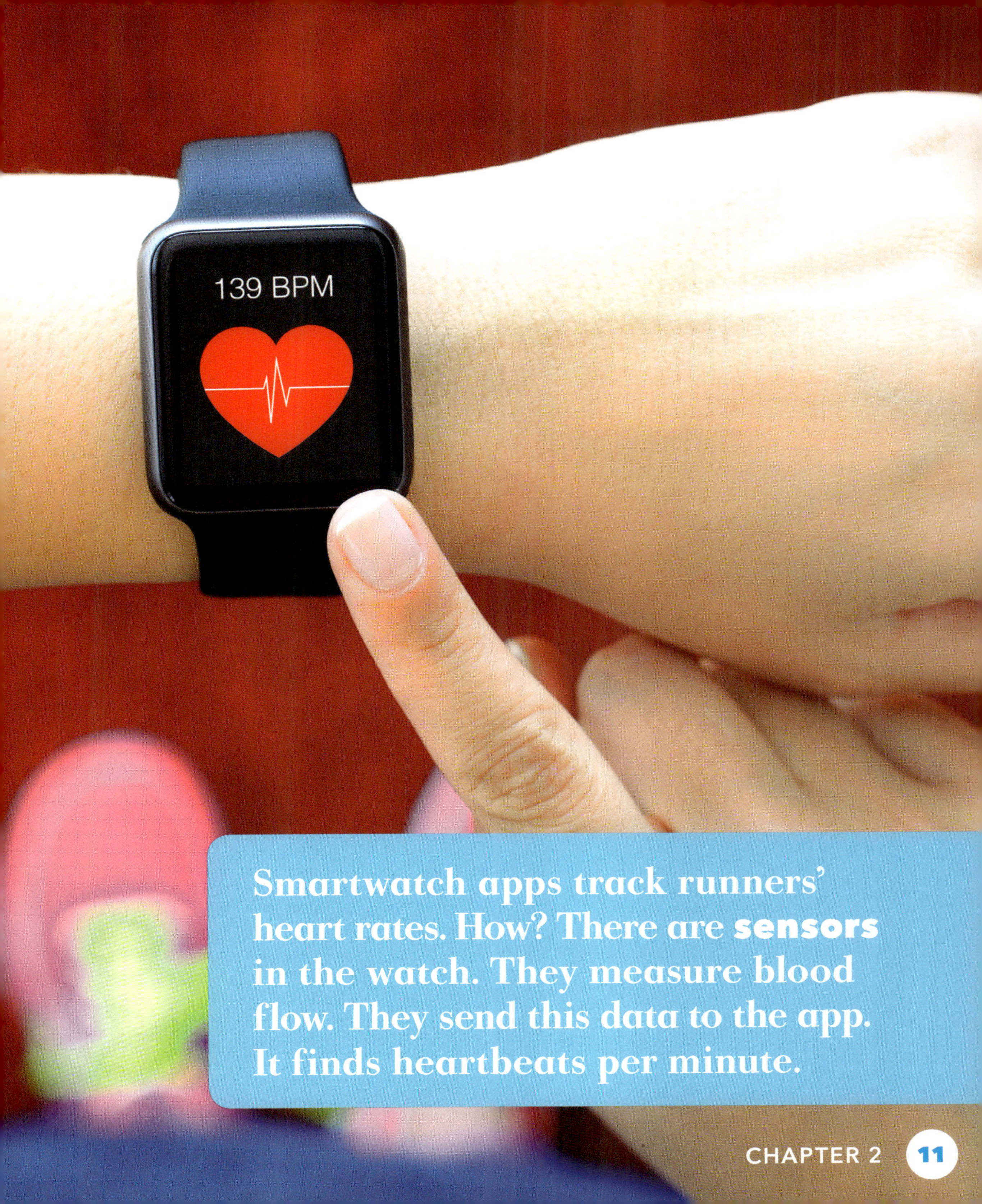

Smartwatch apps track runners' heart rates. How? There are **sensors** in the watch. They measure blood flow. They send this data to the app. It finds heartbeats per minute.

Are you lost? Use a mapping app! It can help you find your way. How? It uses **GPS**. Your phone connects to **satellites**. They send your position to your device.

DID YOU KNOW?

Mobile apps use the GPS built into your device. They can use other features, too. They can connect to cameras, microphones, or contacts.

TRUE-H 3G
6:16 PM
96%
Washington
North Bethesda
Calverton
Cabin John
Bethesda
Silver Spring
Adelphi
College Park
Hyattsville
Washington
Arlington
CAPITOL HILL
SOUTHEAST WASHINGTON
Alexandria
Groveton
Oxon Hill-Glassmanor
Washington
Washington, DC, USA
Route

99%
10:10 AM
SECURE
PAYMENT
ENTER
(click here for more information)

We can use apps to shop online. Apps keep payments safe. How? They **encrypt** your data.

Mobile banking apps use passwords to keep users safe. These apps often ask security questions. Like what? "What is your pet's name?" could be one! With mobile banking apps, we can bank from anywhere. You can even take a picture to deposit a check.

CHAPTER 3

THE FUTURE OF APPS

We connect to smartphones, computers, and even cars and washing machines. Experts think that more than 26 million devices will be connected by 2020. What else do you think will connect?

This huge **network** is called the **Internet of Things**. These devices have built-in sensors. They have **Wi-Fi** connections. Apps connect them all.

The Internet of Things can change daily life. You can run a house with apps! Cold? Turn up the heat with a smart **thermostat**. Turn off lights from another room. Run a robot vacuum from miles away.

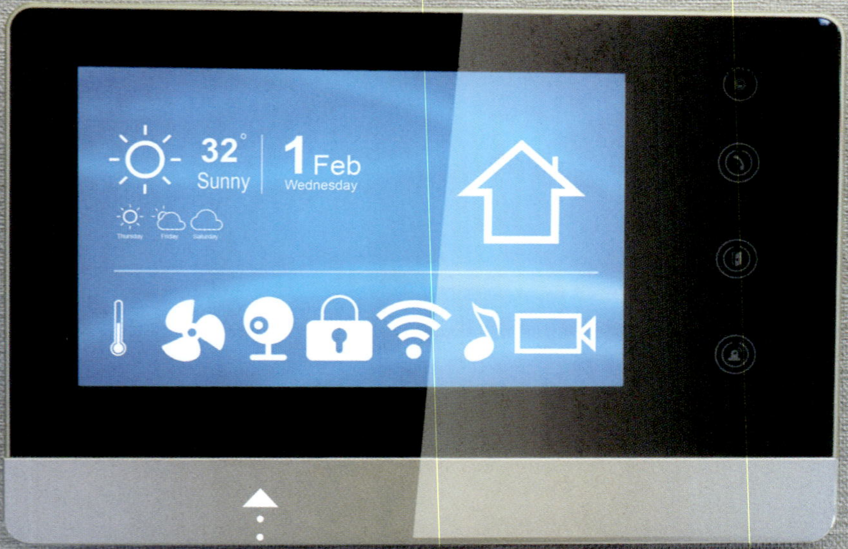

smart thermostat

TAKE A LOOK!

Smart devices in homes are part of the Internet of Things. What can you control with apps? Take a look!

Apps may soon connect to all of your car's settings. Unlock the doors. Honk the horn. Flash the lights. Find your parked car. You could control it all from your device. Apps may even replace car keys.

What do you want to do? There's probably an app for it! If not, maybe you can develop one!

ACTIVITIES & TOOLS

TRY THIS!

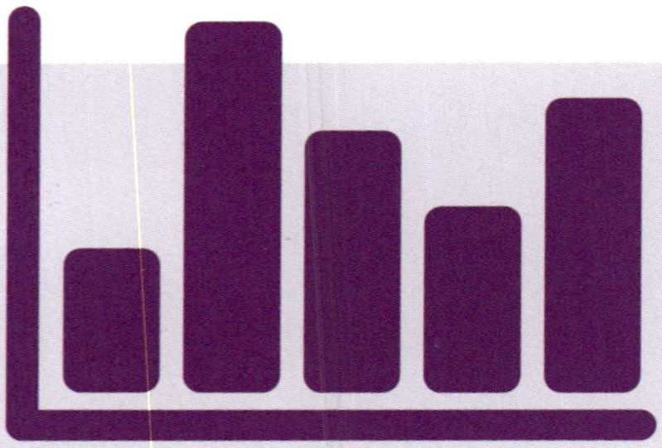

GRAPH APP USE

What apps do your family and friends use? Find out and graph the results!

What You Need:

- two pieces of paper
- pencil
- crayons or colored pencils
- straight edge or ruler

1. Ask 10 friends and family members: Which app do you use the most each day? Write down their responses. Count how often each app was mentioned.
2. Make a chart! Draw a vertical line along the left side of your paper. Draw a horizontal line along the bottom of your paper. Connect it to the vertical line.
3. Number your vertical line from 0 to the largest number from Step 1.
4. Along the bottom line on your paper, write each app name.
5. Draw a vertical box above each app name up to the number you totaled for each app from Step 1.
6. Color in the boxes. Which apps do your family and friends use the most?

GLOSSARY

app: Short for application; a computer program that does specific tasks and is designed for mobile devices.

code: Step-by-step programming statements, written in a coding language, that tell a computer what to do.

data: Information collected in a place so something can be done with it.

developer: Someone who creates software and apps by writing code and debugging it.

encrypt: To shield information so it cannot be read by others.

GPS: A global positioning system that uses satellites to send location signals.

Internet of Things: The connection of devices and objects over the internet, allowing them to send and receive data and communicate with one another.

mobile devices: Devices, such as smartphones and tablets, that can be moved or carried from one place to another.

network: A group of connected devices.

operating systems: Software systems that run all of a computer's memory, processes, software, and hardware.

satellites: Machines that orbit Earth and send and receive signals.

sensors: Devices that collect data and transmit it to devices.

software programs: Computer programs that control the workings of a device or piece of equipment and direct it to do specific tasks.

thermostat: A device that controls furnaces, refrigerators, air conditioners, and other heating and cooling systems.

Wi-Fi: A wireless signal that allows computers and other devices to connect to the internet wherever a signal is available.

INDEX

app stores 6, 9
cars 16, 20
code 9
data 10, 11, 15
developer 9
download 6, 9
encrypt 15
GPS 12
internet 6
Internet of Things 17, 18, 19
lights 18, 19, 20
mapping app 4, 12
mobile banking 15
mobile devices 5
network 17
operating systems 6
satellites 12
sensors 11, 17
smartphones 5, 16
smart thermostat 18
smartwatches 5, 11
software programs 5
vacuum 18, 19
Wi-Fi 17

TO LEARN MORE

Finding more information is as easy as 1, 2, 3.

1. Go to www.factsurfer.com
2. Enter "whatareapps?" into the search box.
3. Choose your book to see a list of websites.

FACT SURFER